To Laura and "Ellie," to John and "Harry," and to the laughter and
love and wonder they brought us each and every day.
                                                    —A. G.

For Jackson, with love
And special thanks to Kathy and Loraine
                                                    —J. B.

I've Got an Elephant

written by
Anne Ginkel

illustrated by
Janie Bynum

I've got an elephant who sleeps in my bed
In Superman pajamas that are yellow, blue, and red.
Though other kids have teddy bears to cuddle up tight,
I've got an elephant to hug me every night.

But when I go to school, he gets lonely and then...

He goes out and brings home an elephant friend.

I've got two elephants who come with me to school.
The kids on the bus all think we're really cool.

They know their ABC's and can count to ten by two's,
They help me with my reading if I ever get confused.

But when I go shopping they get lonely and then...

They go out and bring home an elephant friend.

I've got three elephants who run through the mall
Making stops at all the shops they love the best of all.
They wriggle into fancy shoes and try on every dress.
Sometimes I have to scold them 'cause they make an awful mess.

But when I go swimming, they get lonely and then...

They go out and bring home an elephant friend.

I've got four elephants who swim in the pool.
They're really good at backstroke as a general rule.

They splash each other silly when it gets too hot.
A cool spray of water really hits the spot.

But when I go to ballet, they get lonely and then...

They go out and bring home an elephant friend.

I've got five elephants who dance so gracefully.
They've learned how to point their toes and
    how to bend their knees.
My ballet teacher says that they make a pretty sight
In their pretty pink tutus and their ballerina tights.

But when I go to movies, they get lonely and then...

They go out and bring home an elephant friend.

I've got six elephants who love the movies so.
They get drinks and popcorn to munch on at the show.

If the movie gets too scary, then they hide their little eyes
With their big, floppy ears, and cry elephant cries.

But when I go fishing, they get lonely and then...

They go out and bring home an elephant friend.

I've got seven elephants who fish so patiently.
They sit together on the bank as quiet as can be.
They hardly make a sound. They never breathe a word.
Elephants in fishing hats! It's really quite absurd!

But when I go play dress-up, they get lonely and then...

They go out and bring home an elephant friend.

I've got eight elephants
  who prance down the stairs,
Pretending they are royalty
  and putting on airs.

They gather round the table for a royal English tea,
Sipping from their teacups and having fun with me.

But when I go sledding,
      they get lonely and then...

They go out and bring home an elephant friend.

I've got nine elephants who share my little sled,
With two sturdy runners that are painted bright red.
We sit by the window and wait for it to snow,
Then we climb on that sled and down the hill we go!

But when I take a bath, they get lonely and then...

They go out and bring home an elephant friend.

ENOUGH!

I've got ten elephants who live in the zoo
With a tiger, a crocodile, and twenty kangaroos.

I visit them on Sundays and bring them things to eat,
Popcorn and pizza and a special peanut treat.

But when I get lonely, I go out and then...

I find another playmate.
I make another friend.

Ω

Published by
PEACHTREE PUBLISHERS
1700 Chattahoochee Avenue
Atlanta, Georgia 30318-2112

www.peachtree-online.com

ISBN 1-56145-373-0

Text © 2006 by Anne Ginkel
Illustrations © 2006 by Janie Bynum

Illustrations created in watercolor (on Fabriano Uno Soft Press) and digital pastel

Title typeset in Whimsey ICG Bold from Image Club Graphics, Inc., and text
typeset in Minya Nouvelle by Ray Larabie

Book design by Janie Bynum and Loraine Joyner
Typesetting by Melanie McMahon Ives

Printed in Singapore
10 9 8 7 6 5 4 3 2 1
First Edition

Library of Congress Cataloging-in-Publication Data

Ginkel, Anne.
   I've got an elephant / written by Anne Ginkel ; illustrated by Janie Bynum.-- 1st ed.
     p. cm.
  Summary: Content with one elephant then pleased to have two, a girl begins having
problems as her lonely pachyderms bring home more and more friends throughout
this rhyming counting book.
  ISBN 1-56145-373-0
  [1. Elephants--Fiction. 2. Humorous stories. 3. Stories in rhyme. 4. Counting.] I. Title:
I've got an elephant. II. Bynum, Janie, ill. III. Title.
  PZ8.3.G4327Ive 2006
  [E]--dc22

2006000628